MW01015719

THE WOLF WHO

LOVED MUSIC

Written by CHRISTOPHE GALLAZ

Illustrated by MARSHALL ARISMAN

Creative Editions

MANKATO

Text copyright © 2003 by Christophe Gallaz

Illustrations copyright © 2003 by Marshall Arisman

Original edition: *Le Loup qui aimait la musique*,

extract from *Contes et légendes de Suisse*

© 1996, Editions Nathan, Paris, France

Published in 2003 by Creative Editions, 123 South Broad Street, Mankato,

MN 56001 USA. Creative Editions is an imprint of The Creative Company.

Designed by Rita Marshall.

All rights reserved. No part of the contents of this book may be

reproduced by any means without the written permission of the publisher.

Peter and the Wolf by Serge Prokofiev. Copyright © 1937 (Renewed)

by G. Schirmer, Inc. (ASCAP). International copyright secured.

All rights reserved. Reprinted by permission.

Printed in Italy.

Library of Congress Cataloging-in-Publication Data

Gallaz, Christophe, 1948–

The wolf who loved music / by Christophe Gallaz; illustrated by Marshall Arisman;

translated by Mary Logue.

Summary: After mentioning that she may have seen a wolf in the woods,

a young girl is saddened when police and hunters kill the beast

that she thinks was attracted by her violin playing.

ISBN 1-56846-178-X

[1. Wolves—Fiction. 2. Violin—Fiction. 3. Switzerland—Fiction.]

I. Logue, Mary. II. Title. PZ7.G13634 Wo 2003 [Fic]—dc21 2002074167

First Edition 5 4 3 2 1

This is the story of a little girl. No one is sure whether this is an old story or if it happened recently. But it really doesn't matter.

The girl's name was Anne. She was eight or nine years old, had no brothers or

sisters, and lived with her parents in a large, remote farmhouse on the edge of

a forest. The forest covered nearly all of the Jura mountains in Switzerland,

near Chaux-de-Fonds, above Neuchâtel and Basel.

For some time, Anne had been learning to play the violin. An old professor

came to her house each week. His fingers shook a bit as he showed her how to

string the violin, rub the bow on a block of resin, place her fingers, and pull

the bow across the strings. She didn't know how to read music, but she didn't

mind. She loved simply making the sounds that sprang from her instrument.

One day, Anne asked her mother to tell her a story. Her mother took a

book down from the bookshelf and opened it. There was a picture on the first

page. A picture of a little girl. The girl was wearing a red hood and cloak. She

held a basket in her hands as she walked through a forest.

On the second page of the book was an animal. Anne's mother told her

it was a wolf. Then she read the story. At the end, she explained that the wolf

ate the little girl in the book. And that before eating the little girl, it ate her

grandmother.

Anne didn't believe it.

The next day, Anne woke up very early and slipped down the stairs.

She wandered through the hallway of the main floor and opened the door. Not

making a sound, she went out into the courtyard. It was a beautiful summer

morning, and no one was about. Everyone was still sleeping. She looked

around, then crossed the courtyard, her violin tucked under her arm.

When she reached a field, she watched her shoes walk through the

grass. Certain blades of grass had teeth. Others looked like ears. Others like

hair. Still others looked like arrows. On the far side of the field, she found a

nicely cleared path. It was covered with dust. She took it and entered the forest.

It was darker among the trees. There was moss growing on the ground.

There were brambles. Anne had to lift up her feet to avoid tripping on tree

roots. The trunks of the pine trees were the same gray color as elephants' skin,

but they had scales like old crocodiles. The trunks were all thinner at the top

and ended like matchsticks, covered with green plumage.

Anne walked a long way before coming to a clearing. It was brighter

there than in the forest, but a little darker than the courtyard had been. In the

middle of the clearing was a pond. And dragonflies. They looked like funny

little whirligigs and landed on reeds.

Anne saw a small rock in front of her. It was shaped like a footstool, so

she sat down on it.

Eventually, the light dimmed around Anne. She didn't like to be alone

too long. She put her violin case on the ground, opened it, and took out the

violin. Imitating the old professor, she tightened the strings and rubbed the

resin against the bow. She pulled the bow across the strings. The violin sang.

Anne saw a gray shape. Then night fell.

Anne was very tired and wanted to go to sleep. She slipped down off

the rock. The pine needles on the ground smelled good.

Anne's parents looked for her all day long. They searched every room in

the house. They went into the courtyard, into the field, and onto the dusty path.

Along with their neighbors and many policemen, Anne's parents criss-

crossed the forest for hours. They spent the whole night there. With their

flashlights, they looked in the bottom of the ravines, under the pines, and in

clearings. They called her name, but no one answered them. They found nothing.

Then, just before dawn, they found her. She was sleeping at the foot of

a small rock, her violin next to her. When they woke her, she looked at them,

wondering what they were doing there. She put her violin back in its case.

One of the policemen bent down. He called his colleagues over. They

had discovered animal tracks. The tracks went in a circle around the rock. The

policemen were stunned. They approached Anne and asked her if she had seen

anything before falling asleep. She said no, except the dragonflies in the clear-

ing. They asked her if she had seen a wolf. She remembered the gray shape.

Then she remembered the book. She thought that wolves must love music. She

told them what she had seen. The policemen and the neighbors were quiet.

Everyone went back to the house.

The policemen returned to the forest the next morning, very early.

There were more of them this time. There were also hunters who had come

from all over Switzerland. Many of them were from Valais. They were hunters

who knew a lot about wolves.

The men had rifles and dogs. They pulled out their maps and made

plans. Then they divided themselves into groups, each taking an area. From

time to time, dogs barked. A few hours later, the men gathered again. No one

had seen the wolf. It was noon.

The policemen and the hunters opened their lunches. They ate rye

bread and dried meat. They drank white wine and laughed. They rested for a

little while before re-forming into groups and going out to hunt again.

As evening approached, rifle shots echoed through the forest. The dogs

barked again. Anne was out in the courtyard. There were clouds in the sky.

They stretched over the roof of the farmhouse and trailed off into the forest.

They didn't move. They had a touch of red in them. As the wind blew through

the grass, the clouds turned pale blue, then deep blue.

All of the cars arrived back at the farmhouse at nearly the same

moment, honking their horns. They came in single file down the road, their

headlights shining. The lights jumped around. Sometimes they lit up part of

the farm, then a bit of the field, then back to the farm, then a stretch of the

road. Anne was afraid.

The cars entered the courtyard, and their motors went silent. The

policemen and the hunters got out. The doors slammed. Everyone talked at the

same time. Then someone walked to the back of one of the cars and asked for

help. Two men leaned down into the trunk and pulled out something. An ani-

mal. It didn't move. It was dead. They had bound up its feet. They carried it to

the doorway of the farmhouse and threw it on the ground.

Everyone went to look at it.

First Anne saw the paws. They were thin and very fine. They seemed

dry and delicate, almost like old leaves. Then she saw the stomach. She felt like

touching it. Like laying her head on it. The hair on its back was very dark,

almost black. Then she looked at the head. It seemed sad. The mouth wasn't

quite closed. She could see the front teeth. There was dirt on the muzzle.

Something leaked from the eyes, which, like the mouth, were not quite closed.

The policemen and the hunters gathered around it, their faces red.

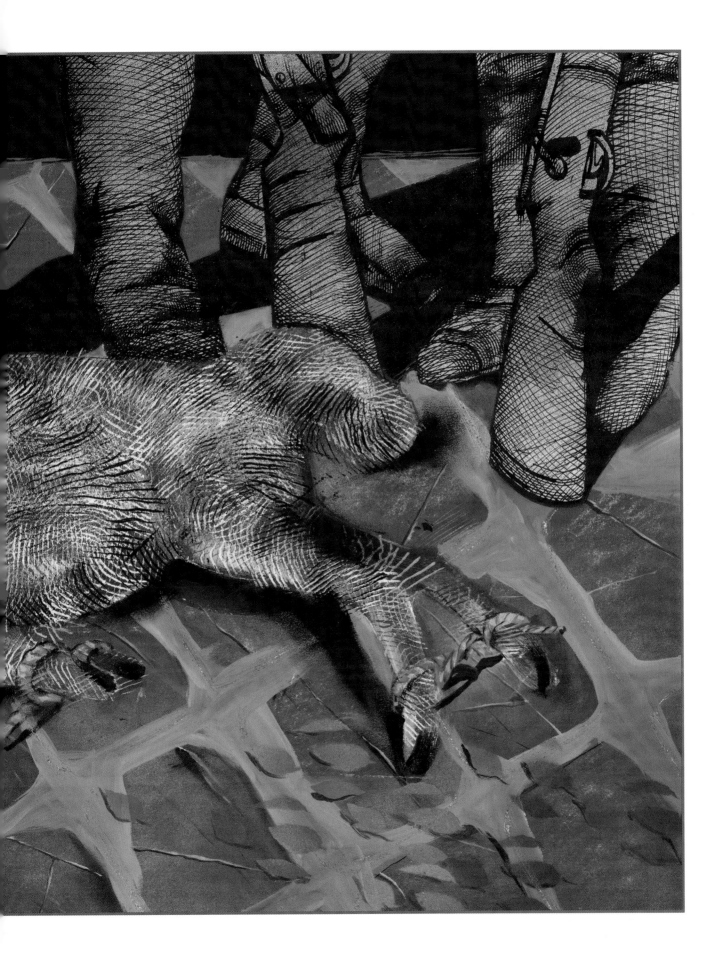

They talked loudly. It was difficult to understand anything they said. They

wore big shoes. Some of them wore boots. They were quite happy as they patted

each other on the shoulders.

Twenty or thirty years have passed. Anne is no longer a little girl. Her parents

have grown old and died. She still lives on the big farm, on the edge of the for-

est that covers nearly all of the Jura mountains in Switzerland, near Chaux-de-

Fonds, above Neuchâtel and Basel.

Every day she takes a long walk, crossing the courtyard, the field, the

path, the forest, the clearing. She goes to the small rock and retraces her steps.

She sees the long clouds in the sky, which stretch out like ribbons. At first a bit

red, then nearly blue, then quite dark. She sees the paws, the stomach, the

hairs on the back, the head. Something leaking from the eyes.

What brutes, what sadness, what sweetness, what solitude.

She takes out her violin and plays.